THE AMERICAN GIRLS

17  64

KAYA, an adventurous Nez Perce girl whose deep love
for horses and respect for nature nourish her spirit

17  74

FELICITY, a spunky, spritely colonial girl,
full of energy and independence

18  24

JOSEFINA, an Hispanic girl whose heart and
hopes are as big as the New Mexico sky

18  54

KIRSTEN, a pioneer girl of strength and
spirit who settles on the frontier

18  64

ADDY, a courageous girl determined to be
free in the midst of the Civil War

19  04

SAMANTHA, a bright Victorian beauty, an
orphan raised by her wealthy grandmother

19  34

KIT, a clever, resourceful girl facing the
Great Depression with spirit and determination

19  44

MOLLY, who schemes and dreams on the
home front during World War Two

1764
KAYA AND LONE DOG

A Friendship Story

BY JANET SHAW

ILLUSTRATIONS BILL FARNSWORTH

VIGNETTES SUSAN MCALILEY

American Girl®

Published by Pleasant Company Publications
Copyright © 2002 by Pleasant Company
All rights reserved. No part of this book may be used or reproduced
in any manner whatsoever without written permission except in the
case of brief quotations embodied in critical articles and reviews.
For information, address: Book Editor, Pleasant Company Publications,
8400 Fairway Place, P.O. Box 620998, Middleton, WI 53562.

Visit our Web site at **americangirl.com**

Printed in China.
02 03 04 05 06 07 08 LEO 12 11 10 9 8 7 6 5 4 3 2

The American Girls Collection®, Kaya™, and American Girl®
are trademarks of Pleasant Company.

PICTURE CREDITS
The following individuals and organizations have generously given
permission to reprint images contained in "Looking Back":

pp. 74–75—Idaho State Historical Society, Boise (neg. 714) (baby in cradleboard); Northwest
Museum of Arts & Culture/Eastern Washington State Historical Society, Spokane, WA
(cradleboard on horse pommel); Idaho State Historical Society (detail, neg. 705) (elder with
child); Idaho State Historical Society (neg. 63-221.25) (sweatlodge); pp. 76–77—Idaho State
Historical Society (neg. 78-203.68) (digging camas roots); courtesy of Grant County Public Utility
District, Moses Lake, WA (lead root gatherers in ceremonial dress); Idaho State Historical Society
(detail, neg. 77-60.22) (Delia Lowry); pp. 78–79—Smithsonian Institution, National
Anthropological Archives (neg. 56,805) (girl on horseback); University of Wyoming Libraries
(F592.D86 1997) (children with puppies); Idaho State Historical Society (neg. 60-179.3)
(elder with puppy); Lewiston Tribune, Lewiston, ID (wolf making school visit).

Library of Congress Cataloging-in-Publication Data

Cataloging-in-Publication Data available from Library of Congress

FOR MY DAUGHTER, KRIS,
HER HUSBAND, PAUL, AND THEIR
SONS, WILL AND PETER,
WITH LOVE

Kaya and her family are *Nimíipuu*, known today as Nez Perce Indians. They speak the Nez Perce language, so you'll see some Nez Perce words in this book. Kaya is short for the Nez Perce name *Kaya'aton'my'*, which means "she who arranges rocks." You'll find the meanings and pronunciations of these and other Nez Perce words in the glossary on pages 80 and 81.

Table of Contents

KAYA'S FAMILY

TOE-TA
Kaya's father, an expert horseman and wise village leader.

EETSA
Kaya's mother, who is a good provider for her family and her village.

KAYA
An adventurous girl with a generous spirit.

BROWN DEER
Kaya's sister, who is old enough to court.

WING FEATHER AND SPARROW
Kaya's mischievous twin brothers.

PI-LAH-KA
AND KAUTSA
*Eetsa's parents, who
guide and comfort Kaya.*

TWO HAWKS
*A Salish boy who is
staying with Kaya's
family.*

LONE DOG
*A special dog who
becomes Kaya's friend.*

A STARVING DOG

As Kaya helped her mother and grandmother set up the tepee poles and cover
them with tule mats, she heard the *honk!
honk! honk!* of geese flying high overhead. She stopped
work, shaded her eyes, and gazed up into the deep
blue sky. Flocks of geese, swans, herons, and cranes
were flying northward from their wintering grounds
in the south. As she listened to the noisy chorus of
their cries, she heard other sounds, too. The warm
spring wind gusted across the rolling hills, rustling
the greening prairie grasses. Larks and swallows
called softly while they built their nests. Her bothersome little brothers laughed and squealed as they
scampered about with the other children. She heard

her grandfather sigh with pleasure when he tilted
up his face to the warm sun that eased the aches
in his bones. Everything Kaya heard joined
in the song of new life returning to the land.

After the long, cold winter, Kaya and her
family had left the sheltered canyons of Salmon
River Country and journeyed upland to dig fresh
kouse roots, the delicious, nourishing food
her people needed. This spring they'd come
to the beautiful Palouse Prairie, where
they'd met *Nimíipuu* and other peoples with
whom they shared these root fields. There
would be many reunions with friends, and much
trading, dancing, games, and horse racing, too. But
Kaya's family had chosen to come here for another
reason—they'd promised to help Two Hawks, the
boy who had escaped with Kaya from enemies
while in Buffalo Country. He needed to get back to
his own people, the *Salish*. Salish often came to the
Palouse Prairie to dig roots and trade. A trader
might take Two Hawks to his home. Kaya looked
around for Two Hawks. He was herding horses
with some other boys. She thought he looked
happy, but she knew he badly missed his family.

2

Her grandmother touched Kaya's arm. Kaya started. She'd let her attention wander.

"Why are you watching the boys when you should be working?" *Kautsa* asked. Her usually gentle voice was stern. "And you're frowning. What have I taught you about making yourself ready to dig roots?"

"You've told me not to have bad thoughts that might make the roots hide themselves," Kaya said. "And I must stay away from sad thoughts, too, so the roots won't make us sick when we eat them."

"*Aa-heh*," Kautsa said. "You must have a pure heart to do your work well and be worthy of your namesake."

Kaya knew her grandmother was right, but she'd found that staying away from bad or sad thoughts was very, very difficult. Her younger sister, Speaking Rain, was still a captive of enemies from Buffalo Country. Kaya's horse had been captured, too, and then traded away. And each time Kaya thought of Swan Circling's death, she had to fight to keep her heart from aching. Swan Circling had been a respected warrior woman, and she had

3

wanted Kaya to have her name, the greatest gift
a person could give. Kaya hoped that one day
she'd feel ready to use it. Sometimes, just for a
moment, Kaya wished she could be a carefree
child again, like her twin brothers, who were
happily trying to sneak up on green racers and
catch the little snakes with their bare hands.

"Will the root digging begin soon?"
Kaya asked.

"Very soon!" Kautsa said with a
smile. "Two women elders went to check
the fields today. They came back with good
news. The roots are waiting for us. The roots are
singing!"

Kaya felt a shiver down her back. *Hun-ya-wat*,
the Creator, sent both animals and plants so that
Nimíipuu might have food to live. But if anyone
treated these gifts disrespectfully, then the fish,
the deer, the berries, or the roots might not give
themselves to The People. Kaya prayed that
nothing she had said or done—or thought—
would cause her people to go hungry.

Kautsa put her strong arm around Kaya's
shoulder. "I see that something troubles you,

Granddaughter." Now she spoke gently, as if she understood Kaya's troubled thoughts.

"I still have a lot of sadness in me," Kaya admitted. "Do you think I should keep away from the digging?"

"Only you know your own heart," Kautsa said.

"I want to work with you and the others!" Kaya blurted. "I want to do my part, like my namesake always did."

"Of course you do!" Kautsa said. She squeezed Kaya to her, then held her at arm's length to look at her. "But you've told me your heart is troubled. For now, let others work with the food until your dark thoughts leave you and the time of mourning is over in your heart. You can join us when your thoughts are clear again."

"Aa-heh," Kaya said with a sigh. She knew her grandmother's advice was wise, but the realization that she wouldn't be working with the other girls and women made her feel even lonelier.

Kautsa glanced at the sun, high overhead. "We need firewood so I can get our meal started," she said.

"I'll get some," Kaya said at once. She was glad

to walk across the greening field to the stream, which was rushing with the runoff of melted snow. As she went, she saw horses rolling on their backs to shed their thick winter coats. When she bent to pick up driftwood, she saw the first early blooms of yellowbells. Soon her thoughts were lighter, but still she felt uneasy, as if she were being watched. Were the Stick People peeking at her? Was a bear prowling nearby, hungry after its long winter sleep? She stood and looked around.

Kaya's father had taught her that even the smallest of signs carry big messages. He'd taught her to look for the tip of a deer's antler, or the tremble of a branch after an elk has passed. So Kaya let her gaze move slowly across the scrub brush, searching for any little sign of what might be hidden there. In a moment, she saw the amber glint of two eyes watching her through the leaves. Those eyes reminded her of something—what? Then she remembered the yellow eyes of the wolf that had led her through the snowstorm toward her father when she was stranded on the Buffalo Trail. But a wolf wouldn't come so close to where

people camped. She crouched. Now she made out a pale muzzle and a black nose, the head of a large dog.

Drawn by the dog's searching gaze, Kaya inched closer. The dog moved slowly out of the bushes toward her, the tip of its tail wagging slightly. She could see scars on its back and shoulders. She could also see its ribs showing plainly, though its belly was swollen with pups soon to be born. It wasn't one of their camp dogs, which she knew well. Perhaps it had come here with another band. But why had it strayed off alone?

Gazing up at Kaya with sad eyes, the dog whined low in its throat.

"Are you asking for food?" Kaya said. "I don't have any for you, but your people will feed you. Go back to them. Go!" When she raised her hand, the dog cowered as though afraid Kaya would strike. "Go!" Kaya repeated.

The dog gazed at Kaya for a long moment, perhaps hoping she'd change her mind. Then it slipped away into the bushes, quickly vanishing from sight.

As soon as the dog disappeared, Kaya had the

sinking feeling that she'd just done a terrible thing. She remembered that when she and her sister were slaves, fed only on scraps, she'd vowed never again to chase off the starving dogs that sometimes appeared at the camp. This hungry dog had asked for her help, but she'd chased it away. Kaya whistled to call the dog back to her side. But it was too late— the lone dog was gone.

On the day chosen for root digging to begin, the lead diggers rose before first light and went to the sweat lodge to cleanse and purify themselves. Kaya's older sister, Brown Deer, was one of the lead diggers this year. Kaya watched as Brown Deer dressed herself in her best

sweat lodge

moccasins and her white deerskin dress decorated with elks' teeth and shell beads. Kautsa set Brown Deer's work hat on her head. By the time the lead diggers reached the root fields, the eastern sky bloomed pink as a prairie rose. Soon Kaya heard the women begin to sing the sacred song of thanks for the gift of new food—the root harvest would be a good one! Kaya knew it was right for her to stay away from the digging, but how she longed to wear her own new work hat and to dig with the other women and girls.

As Kaya prepared a morning meal for the twins, she gazed out over the rolling hills, hoping to see the hungry dog she'd chased off. Every day she'd looked for that lone dog, but she hadn't seen it again. How terrible if it had starved to death!

"Little daughter, I've been looking for you!" *Toe-ta's* deep voice came from behind her. She turned and saw her father gazing kindly at her, as if he understood that she was sad. "I've been thinking that we need to train another horse to pull a travois," he said to her.

"I worked with my namesake when she taught a horse to pull one," Kaya said, always careful not to say the name of the dead aloud.

"*Tawts!*" Toe-ta said. "I can use your help. I think the old gray horse your grandmother used to ride would be a good one to work with. Come with me and we'll put a training harness on it. Bring the twins with you—they can help, too."

Toe-ta tied the gray horse to a bent shrub.

While the boys waited impatiently, Kaya and her
father looped a rawhide rope around the horse's neck.
Long rawhide lines attached to the rope led back to a
dried buffalo hide that rested on the ground a few
feet behind the horse's hind legs. When the training
harness was secure, Toe-ta gestured for Kaya to climb
onto the hide to add weight to the drag. The hide was
back far enough so that if the horse kicked, its legs
wouldn't reach Kaya.

Kaya crawled onto the buffalo hide, sat, and
held onto the lines with both hands. Then Toe-ta led
the horse forward by the halter, speaking all the
while in a low, reassuring voice. But the gray shied
and dodged and started to kick at the unaccustomed
burden it pulled. Kaya laughed as the buffalo hide
bumped and skidded over the smooth ground—this
horse wouldn't toss her off! The twins laughed,
too—they wanted to ride on that swaying rawhide.

After a short time, the horse quieted down and
walked steadily as Toe-ta led it around the ring of
tepees. At last he drew the horse to a halt and
motioned for Kaya to stand up and take the lead-
rope from him. "You boys get on now," he told the
twins, and they eagerly jumped onto the hide as

Kaya took hold of the halter.

Toe-ta watched as Kaya led the gentle horse away from the tepees, the little boys grinning as they hung tightly to the rawhide lines. When Toe-ta was satisfied that the work was going well, he nodded. "In a few days, when the horse is accustomed to the feel of the drag, we'll add travois poles to the harness," he said. "Go slowly, Kaya. Walk around the village a few more times, then put the horse back with the herd."

Kaya knew her father had asked her to help train the horse because she couldn't dig roots with the other women and girls. And her father had been wise—her heart was lighter now. Like Swan Circling, Kaya loved to work with the horses. When the training session was over and she took the harness off the gray, she noticed that one of its rear hooves seemed worn and sore. She resolved to make a rawhide shoe to fill with medicine for that sore hoof—another lesson her namesake had taught her.

⟁

As Kaya walked back to the village from where the horses grazed, she heard a dog growling nearby.

Her father had been wise—her heart was lighter now.
Like Swan Circling, Kaya loved to work with the horses.

The growl was low and challenging. Kaya went through the brush to see what had alarmed the dog.

On the far side of the hill, she came upon Snow Paws, the big black leader of the village dog pack. His hackles were up, his ears were pricked forward, and his teeth were bared. When he saw Kaya approaching, he snarled more fiercely at something backed up against a rocky outcropping. It wouldn't be a skunk—Snow Paws was much too smart for that. What did he have there?

Kaya parted the bushes. There, beside the rocks, was Lone Dog, the one she'd been searching for. Lone Dog's teeth were bared, and she was growling, too, facing off against the big male. With a glance, Kaya saw that Lone Dog's bones showed even more sharply. Hunger must have given her courage, for tough old Snow Paws could drive off any dog that approached. Even now he was beginning to bark, and soon he'd charge at Lone Dog and bite her.

This time Kaya wouldn't lose her chance to help the starving dog. She stepped between the two dogs and shook a stick at the barking Snow Paws. "Leave her alone!" she ordered him. "Get away from her! Go on now, get away!"

Growling, Snow Paws backed up a few steps. Maybe he thought Kaya had given him the wrong command. But when she shook the stick again, he reluctantly turned tail and stalked off, looking back over his shoulder.

When Snow Paws had gone, Kaya crouched, holding out her hand for Lone Dog to sniff. But the dog kept near the rocks, where she'd been digging out a den. She gazed warily at Kaya, as if Kaya might take up the attack where the black dog had left it.

"Here, come here," Kaya crooned. "I won't chase you away again." She reached into the bag on her belt and took out the pieces of dried salmon she carried for a quick meal. She held out the fish to Lone Dog. "Here's a little food for you. Come on, eat it."

Still Lone Dog hesitated, although the scent of fish made her tremble. Her yellow eyes gazed intently into Kaya's.

Kaya placed the fish on the ground and stepped back. "Please, don't be afraid of me. Take the food," she said.

This time Lone Dog didn't need urging.

14

She sprang forward, snapped up the fish, and gulped it down as she bolted away.

Kaya watched Lone Dog round the outcropping and disappear. "I'll bring you more food," she whispered. "You asked me for help and I'll give it. I promise."

Later that day, Kaya sat beside her grandmother as they worked. Kaya held a circle of thick elk hide on her lap. She was lacing a rawhide drawstring through holes she'd punched along the edge of the hide. When she pulled the drawstring tight, she'd have a round moccasin that would fit over the gray horse's hoof and hold a poultice to heal the sore place.

Kautsa was peeling the skins off roots so they could be dried in the sun. She handed Kaya a cleaned root to munch on. Fresh roots were welcome after a season of dried food.

"I have something I want to tell you about a dog," Kaya said.

"You always have stories to tell me," Kautsa said with a smile. With her small stone knife, she peeled off the dark root skins. The pile of pale, clean roots on the tule mat in front of her was growing quickly. "Is this story about a dog fight?"

Kaya looked closely at her grandmother, who always seemed to know so much. "How did you know about the fight?"

"I have ears!" Kautsa said with a laugh. "What happened, Granddaughter?"

"A lone dog came to our village for food," Kaya said. "The dog's starving, and she's going to have pups soon. I felt sorry for her. Snow Paws tried to chase her away—that's the barking you heard. But I made him stop."

Kautsa nodded, thinking. "Snow Paws has been the leader of our pack for a long time," she reminded Kaya. "He's a wise dog, and a strong-hearted one. You remember how he got his name, don't you? When he was hardly more than a pup, a hunter took him along to hunt elk. It was winter, and an  avalanche crashed down a cliff and buried the man! Snow Paws dug and dug through the snow until he uncovered the hunter. He saved the man's life. A dog like that is one to be trusted. He must have a reason for trying to chase off this lone dog you speak of."

"Snow Paws might think Lone Dog would take his food," Kaya suggested.

"We give our dogs enough to eat," Kautsa said. "If they're hungry, they know how to hunt for more to fill their bellies."

"But Snow Paws chases off every strange dog, doesn't he?" Kaya asked.

"He lets strange dogs join our pack if they accept him as the leader," Kautsa corrected her. "But he chases off dogs that might be dangerous for some reason. Snow Paws senses these things. Perhaps the lone dog is sick, and might make our dogs sick as well."

"Her eyes are bright and her fur's not falling out," Kaya said. "She doesn't look sick—she looks hungry."

"You told me your story to ask what I think about it, didn't you?" Kautsa said. "I think Snow Paws knows more about this lone dog than you do, Granddaughter, that's what I think."

Kaya bit her lip. Her grandmother was wise in all things. But Kaya had given her promise to Lone Dog. As Kaya did so often, she tried to think what Swan Circling would do if she were here. Kaya decided that if Lone Dog wasn't a menace, Swan Circling certainly wouldn't let her starve.

CHAPTER TWO

NEWBORN PUPPIES

The next morning Kaya went to the stream as the first rays of sun struck through the blanket of mist hanging over the water. Sandpipers were stepping along the shoreline, and a raccoon searched for crawfish in the shallows. Kaya dipped in her water basket, then drank from her cupped hand. It was a quiet morning, though she could hear the voices of the boys taking their morning swim downstream.

As Kaya drank, she saw Lone Dog appear on a rise a little distance away, then look around warily as she trotted to the stream to drink. Kaya set down her water basket and waited until Lone Dog

KAYA AND LONE DOG

had drunk her fill. *"Tawts may-we!"* Kaya greeted the dog softly. "Look, here's food for you. I didn't forget." She held out the bone she'd brought with her on the chance she would see the dog.

Lone Dog's ears pricked up and she stood with her head lifted, sniffing all the scents traveling over the water and land. Kaya knew Lone Dog smelled the bone, but she didn't come to take it from Kaya's hand as Kaya had hoped. It wouldn't be easy to earn this dog's trust.

Kaya called again, but this time Lone Dog began to back away. "Don't go," Kaya said. "You need this food."

When Lone Dog hesitated, Kaya put down the bone by the stream. She picked up her water basket and started walking, as if she didn't have a thought for the dog. When she glanced over her shoulder, she saw Lone Dog seize the bone and lope off into the brush with it. In a moment the dog had disappeared.

"Did I just see you feeding a coyote?" Raven called to Kaya. Several other boys laughed. They were running back to the village from their swim, water dripping from their bare arms and their hair.

They were full of the energy that the fresh, cold water had given them.

"You know that wasn't a coyote," Kaya said crossly. She walked faster. She wasn't in any mood to be teased by these bothersome boys, who swarmed around her like a cloud of gnats.

One of the boys was Fox Tail, who had challenged her to race when they were at *Wallowa*. He gave her a sly grin. "You say it's not a coyote, but it acts like one," he insisted. "Coyotes travel alone, but dogs stay with their pack."

"And it should be guarding the camp," Raven added. "Our dogs are supposed to protect us. That's their job. You shouldn't reward a lazy dog with a bone!"

"My people would chase off a dog that didn't do its work," Two Hawks added. He was one of the gang now.

Kaya gave Two Hawks an angry glance—it wasn't fair that he would criticize her after all they'd been through together. "When that dog gets used to us, she'll join our pack," she said. "You'll see."

"We'll see her get fat on our food, then go her own way!" Raven insisted.

"Aa-heh! Now I know why Kaya likes that dog!" Fox Tail cried. "She likes it because it thinks only of itself—just like a magpie! Isn't that right, Magpie?" He swung around and walked backward, so he could see Kaya's burning face as he taunted her.

It took all of Kaya's self-control to keep herself from giving Fox Tail a swat—or letting a tear slide from her eye. Would she never outgrow that awful nickname she'd gotten when she failed to take care of the twins? Would the others never forget that it was her fault they'd all been switched? Fiercely, she bit the inside of her lip so that she wouldn't let her anger, or her disappointment, show.

"No one can tame a coyote—or a wolf!" Fox Tail said. "Some girls can't tame a dog, either!" With that, the laughing boys bounded off.

You're all skunks! Kaya thought. Fighting to be calm—and to have good thoughts—she trudged back to the camp.

Each day when all the women and girls went to dig roots, Kaya put the harness on the gray horse and trained it to pull the buffalo-hide drag. Its sore hoof was healing well, and soon she was able to add lightweight poles to the harness. The gentle horse began to learn to pull those, too. As Kaya worked with the horse, her mind was on Lone Dog. Would she ever come to trust Kaya?

Kaya looked for Lone Dog every time she went to the stream. She waited on the shore as long as she could, but Lone Dog didn't appear. Where was she? Perhaps Lone Dog had already moved on, as the boys had said she would. The thought that Lone Dog might leave made Kaya sad. With her sister in captivity, Kaya often felt alone—like the dog. She realized she wanted the dog to become her friend.

One morning, as Kaya gazed at the empty shoreline, a thought came to her—perhaps Lone Dog was working on the den she'd begun on the hillside. After Kaya took the water basket she had filled to her tepee, she went looking for that place again.

Kaya was almost upon the den before she saw it. Lone Dog had hollowed out a deep circle beneath a rocky overhang. When Kaya crouched, she made out Lone Dog's yellow eyes gazing over the top of the nest, her face barely visible through the long grass.

"Tawts may-we," Kaya said gently. "I thought

23

"What a good mother you are . . . Here, you must be hungry, too."

I might find you here." She slowly went closer, hoping not to scare off the dog. Lone Dog watched her come. She wasn't wary, or nervous.

Kaya got down on her stomach and looked into the nest where Lone Dog lay. There, snuggled up next to one another against their mother's side, were four little newborn puppies. They were nursing, their paws pushing at their mother's belly. With their stubby legs and big bellies, they looked to Kaya more like ground squirrels than like dogs.

Panting heavily, Lone Dog gazed up steadily into Kaya's eyes. She seemed calm and sure of herself now that she'd given birth to her pups.

"What a good mother you are!" Kaya whispered to her. She watched the puppies nurse a little longer, then placed the food she'd brought at the edge of the nest. "Here, you must be hungry, too."

Lone Dog sniffed the meaty bone, then shifted herself and got to her feet so she could eat. When she stood, the puppies lost their hold on her and squealed as they tumbled onto their sides. Their eyes weren't open yet, but they found one another by the warmth of their bodies and crept close together to fall fast asleep.

Lying beside the nest, Lone Dog began to gnaw on the bone. Suddenly, her ears pricked up and she began to growl.

Kaya looked around. She didn't see anything. "It's all right," she said soothingly. "Your pups are safe."

But now Lone Dog was on her feet, her hackles raised along her back and her tail lifted straight up. She growled again, then lunged partway up the hillside, barking ferociously.

Kaya jumped up, too. Was a cougar after the helpless pups?

Instead of a cat, Kaya saw Snow Paws stalking along the top of the hill. Maybe he was only investigating the new scents, but sometimes male dogs went after newborn pups. He must not harm Lone Dog or her little ones! "Get away! Get!" Kaya commanded him. Lone Dog continued to bark violently to keep him at bay.

Snow Paws bared his teeth, as if he were about to charge Lone Dog. Then he changed his mind. He snarled and began backing off. He didn't want a fight with this fiercely protective mother—or with Kaya, who had seized a thick stick and was shaking it at him.

Even after Snow Paws disappeared, Lone Dog continued to bark. Only when she was satisfied that the intruder was gone did she return to her nest. The puppies had slept peacefully through all the commotion. Gnawing the bone, Lone Dog lay down beside them again.

"Aa-heh, you know how to take care of your pups," Kaya murmured to her. "I'll come visit you again soon."

"These willow branches must be carried down to the streamside," Kautsa said to Kaya and Brown Deer. "We need to build a larger sweat lodge." She handed the girls bundles of willows and took one on her own back. They walked downhill to the bank of the stream, where Kaya's mother was hollowing out a shallow pit in the gravel.

Each day, in winter as well as summer, Kaya and the other girls and women bathed in a sweat lodge. The men and boys did the same. Sweat baths relaxed them and made them clean and healthy in both body and spirit.

Kautsa set to work bending willow branches to

form a dome over the pit. Brown Deer and Kaya followed her lead, placing the branches so that they followed the four directions. The girls often helped to build a lodge like this one—they put up sweat lodges everywhere they stayed.

"Why are you gazing at the hills instead of doing your work, Daughter?" *Eetsa* asked Kaya. "Here, hold these willows so I can tie them together."

"I was thinking about Lone Dog," Kaya admitted to her mother. "I found the den she made in the hillside."

"It's too bad that dog doesn't come to live with us," Eetsa said. "She could help guard our camp."

"That's what the boys told me," Kaya said. "They teased me about Lone Dog. They said she thinks only of herself—like a magpie. Like *me*, they meant. They won't let me forget that nickname." Swan Circling had promised that the nickname wouldn't matter so much when Kaya got older—but that day seemed a long time coming.

Kautsa stood upright to rub her sore back with both hands. "Don't you remember the story of how dogs, wolves, and coyotes came to be as they are, Granddaughter?"

"I *think* I remember," Kaya said.

"It's an old, old story," Kautsa went on, weaving and tying willows into the framework again. "Four brothers were roaming the hills together. They were looking everywhere for food, because they were very hungry. When they spotted tepees in a valley, and smelled meat cooking, one of the brothers went down for a closer look. People gave him some meat to eat, and he went running back to the other three brothers and told them what had happened. 'If we go live with people, they'll feed us!' he said. 'We won't go hungry anymore.'

"But the other three brothers didn't agree with him. Two of them said, 'If people feed you, they'll expect you to work hard for them in return. We'd rather go off together and hunt for our own food.' The other brother said, 'I don't need people at all, and I don't need companions, either. I'll go hunt by myself.'

"So the first brother became a dog, and chose to eat our food and do our work," Kautsa continued. "The brother who went off to live all by himself became a coyote. And the two brothers who chose to stay together and hunt

coyote

29

as a team became wolves. Remember, Nimíipuu are like wolves. We're strong as individuals, but we always work together. That's how it should be."

"It's not natural for a dog to live all alone," Brown Deer chimed in.

"She's not all alone anymore," Kaya said. "She's had her pups, four of them, like the story. But they'll grow up to be dogs, not coyotes or wolves."

"Daughter, don't be too sure of that," Eetsa warned. She began laying rye grass thickly over the frame to create a covering.

"What do you mean?" Kaya asked.

"I mean I've had a glimpse of that dog," Eetsa said. "She looks to me as if she's got some wolf blood in her. That would be bad, you know. A dog obeys its master, but no man can be master to a wolf. If there's wolf blood in that dog, she might challenge her master. You said you thought Lone Dog had been beaten—maybe that's why."

"Aa-heh," Brown Deer agreed. "She might have bitten a child, or snapped at a baby. She could be dangerous." She laid more armloads of rye grass onto the framework.

"I think you should keep away from Lone Dog," Kautsa said firmly. "I think you should stay with the dogs we're sure we can trust."

Kaya felt a stab of dismay in her chest. "There's something I must ask you," she said in a low voice.

"Aa-heh, ask me anything," Kautsa replied. "I'll answer you as I think best."

"I hope you'll allow me to go on feeding Lone Dog," Kaya said carefully. "I gave her my promise that I would help her. Shouldn't I keep my word to a dog, as well as to a person?"

Kautsa picked up several fir boughs and laid them on the floor of the new sweat lodge. She didn't speak as she spread out the sweet-smelling boughs, and Kaya knew her grandmother was considering how best to answer. She held her breath.

Finally Kautsa straightened up and put her hands on her hips. "I think I understand you, Granddaughter. You want to be someone who always keeps her word, and that is right. You may go on feeding Lone Dog, as you promised you would. But I want you to be very, very careful for any sign that she might bite. Take my warning seriously, Granddaughter."

"I will," Kaya said quickly. She felt the ache in her chest ease.

"Tawts!" Kautsa's stern face softened and her dark eyes sparkled. "Now I'd like you to start piling up stones to use in our sweat lodge. Your mother named you for the first thing she saw after you were born—a woman arranging the stones for a sweat lodge like this one. That's your job today, Kaya'aton'my'. Do it well."

MORE WARNINGS

Every day now, more and more people arrived at the digging fields of the Palouse Prairie. This was a very good place for digging kouse. It was also a very good marketplace for traders. Friends from the north traded skins of bear, beaver, and mink from the mountains where they lived. Friends from the west traded their special cedar bark baskets. In return, Kaya's people traded deer and elk skins and the delicious dried salmon that everyone wanted. And every day Kaya kept a lookout for the arrival of Salish traders—she hoped they'd take Two Hawks back to his family. But, as others arrived, there was no sign of anyone from his country. Weren't they going to come to the Palouse this year?

Kaya visited Lone Dog and her pups every day. Often, as she approached the nest, she found Lone Dog sitting beside it, gazing in her direction. The dog seemed to be waiting for Kaya now. And sometimes it seemed to her that Lone Dog smiled as she ran the back of her hand along the dog's muzzle. "You know I want to be your friend, don't you?" Kaya asked quietly. And Lone Dog wagged her tail as if to say, *Aa-heh, I want to be your friend, too.*

One morning when Kaya was coming back from visiting Lone Dog and her pups, she heard the crier calling out that a new trader had arrived. He had come from far away, where the Big River flows into the sea. Quickly Kaya's grandfather dressed in his best hide shirt and leggings, wrapped his deerskin robe over his shoulder, and went to meet the man. Her grandfather was a shrewd trader. He took with him camas cakes, buffalo hides, and bundles of tules, things that people from the coast would be sure to want.

The Big River meets the sea.

All day Kaya looked forward to *Pi-lah-ka's* return. Her grandfather would have many stories to tell, and he might have heard something about Speaking Rain. Slaves were sometimes traded to other tribes—could her sister have been traded to people from the west?

Pi-lah-ka didn't ride back for a long time. When he did, there were big packs tied onto his pack horses.

Two Hawks was helping Kaya's father coil up hemp rope for trading. Toe-ta and Two Hawks hurried with Kaya and the others to crowd around Pi-lah-ka. Toe-ta motioned for everyone to be seated. Then Pi-lah-ka opened up a pack and showed them what he'd gotten in trade with the man from the coast. First, he handed around a few special beads he'd gotten in exchange for a fine buffalo hide.

Kaya held one of the precious beads in her palm. It gleamed a deep blue, as if she held a piece of the evening sky. Oh, it was beautiful!

Kautsa held up another blue bead to the light. But instead of smiling, she frowned. "These beads are a lovely color," she said slowly. "But I think our bone and shell beads are best for our clothes. I like the old ways."

"For you, old is always better," Pi-lah-ka teased in his deep voice.

"Old ways are safe ways," Kautsa said stubbornly.

Pi-lah-ka took a very small pouch from his bundle and placed it in her lap. "Then here's something that will please you," he said.

Kautsa opened the pouch and lifted out a strand of glistening dentalium shells. As she held up the valuable shells for everyone to admire, her face lit up like sun shining after a storm. "You did well!" she said to Pi-lah-ka.

Brown Deer's face was alight, too. "Some of those shells would be beautiful on a dress!" she exclaimed.

"Aa-heh, on a dress for a young woman who hopes to marry soon!" Kautsa added with a smile. "These shells are just the decorations we need."

"The trader told of many beautiful new things," Pi-lah-ka insisted. "He told of cloth dyed the brightest red he'd ever seen."

Kautsa's eyes grew wide. "Where did he see bright red cloth?" she demanded.

"The trader said men in huge boats—men with pale, hairy faces—had such cloth," Pi-lah-ka admitted.

Kautsa folded her arms over her chest and drew herself up tall. "Listen to me. I want to tell you something," she said in her most serious voice.

Toe-ta gestured for everyone to pay attention. Kaya and Brown Deer put down the beads. The twins stopped whispering to Two Hawks and turned toward their grandmother to hear what she had to say.

When Kautsa had everyone's attention, she began to speak. "One night not long ago, I had a vision. In my vision, I was holding a piece of bright red cloth. Then, as I held it, the red cloth vanished, and my hand was red with blood!" She turned to her husband. "My vision is a warning—harm will come to us from the men with pale faces."

Kaya shivered. Her grandmother had told them her visions before. They were given to her so she could help protect The People.

Pi-lah-ka and Toe-ta nodded solemnly. They always respected Kautsa's visions.

But out of the corner of her eye, Kaya saw Two Hawks turn to look at the arrival of more new traders riding by with their many pack horses. After a moment, he jumped to his feet.

"Sit, Two Hawks," Toe-ta said sternly to him. "Pay attention to your elders."

Two Hawks sat again. Kaya could see that he was trying to be respectful, but he was almost too excited to hold still.

"Tell us," Pi-lah-ka said. "What's troubling you?"

"I think those traders are Salish," Two Hawks said. "They're hauling hide tepee covers like my people use, and I think I recognize that big black horse. Maybe those men know what's happened to my family. Can't we follow them?"

Toe-ta stood up right away. "Get your horse," he told Two Hawks. "Kaya, come with me on my horse. Let's see if these men are Salish." He put his hand on Two Hawks's shoulder. "If they are, we'll trade this boy to them for a worn-out moccasin. That would be an even trade, wouldn't it?"

Two Hawks grinned at Toe-ta's joke. Then his glance caught Kaya's, and his smile dimmed. She saw that he was very happy—and also a little sad. Of course, he wanted to get back to his home again. But now he felt at home with her people, too.

The traders were setting up their camp on the eastern edge of the clusters of tepees. Toe-ta signaled a greeting to them as they rode up. But Two Hawks reined in his horse and circled around behind Toe-ta as if he were feeling shy.

A young trader stepped forward, shading his eyes against the setting sun. Toe-ta threw him the words, *This boy is Salish. Do you know him?*

The trader squinted up at Two Hawks and beckoned for him to ride closer. After a moment, the trader shook his head—it had been a long time since Two Hawks was taken captive, and the man didn't recognize the boy.

But Two Hawks recognized him! He slipped off his horse and ran to the young man. Two Hawks threw his arms around the man's waist and pushed his forehead against his broad shoulder. Then they were both laughing and talking at the same time.

When Kaya and her father joined them, Two Hawks turned to them excitedly. "This is my uncle— my mother's brother!" he cried. "He says my parents are alive and well. My sisters are well, too. He'll take me home with him!"

"Tawts!" Toe-ta said. "Two Hawks, ask your

uncle to share a meal with us. We have much to talk over with him."

✦

Eetsa prepared a meal of kouse mush, berries, and deer meat. Afterward, the men talked. Because Two Hawks spoke both Nimíipuu and the Salish language of his people, he acted as interpreter. Sometimes they used sign language, too.

Kaya closely followed what they said. Two Hawks told of his time as a slave of enemies from Buffalo Country, and of his and Kaya's escape, and how Toe-ta had found them on the Buffalo Trail. Young Uncle told of everything that had happened to Two Hawks's family while he was gone from them. Toe-ta made plans to join some Salish men to hunt buffalo in their country to the east, and they agreed to meet again the next day to trade with each other.

Then Toe-ta asked about Speaking Rain. Had Young Uncle seen or heard of his little daughter, a blind girl? She'd been a captive, too, but she might have escaped, or been traded. Was there any news of her?

Young Uncle frowned sadly. *I have not heard of the girl you describe*, he said with his hands.

Kaya clasped her hands tightly to keep from crying. But now Two Hawks turned to look her in the eye. "You helped me and brought me to my family," he said to her. "I give my word that I'll try to find your sister and bring her to you."

Kaya blinked back her unshed tears. Two Hawks was her friend after all. "*Katsee-yow-yow*," she said to him gratefully.

Then Two Hawks and Young Uncle spoke together for a little while. Two Hawks turned to Toe-ta. "My uncle gives you his pledge, too," he said. "When it's time for salmon fishing at Celilo Falls, some of my people will join your people there. Maybe we'll have news of your daughter then."

Toe-ta nodded. He threw Young Uncle the words, *Thank you for your help.*

Kaya glanced at her mother. Eetsa sat with her head bowed, her lips pressed tightly together. Kaya saw the sadness in her father's face, too. She understood that to lose a child was a terrible thing. And to lose a sister was terrible as well.

Two Hawks leaned toward Kaya. "I asked my uncle about your horse with the star on her forehead," he said. "He hasn't seen your horse, but we'll be on the lookout."

"Katsee-yow-yow," Kaya murmured a second time. Then she got to her feet and moved away from the others.

All the bad news she'd heard tore at her heart, and soon Two Hawks would be leaving, too. Where could she find comfort? She knelt beside her sleeping place and slipped Speaking Rain's buckskin doll out of her pack. As she clutched the doll to her chest, she thought of Lone Dog. She remembered how Lone Dog had licked Kaya's hands when she'd visited her that morning. So Kaya tucked the doll away again, put some scraps of food into her bag, and headed toward the hillside where Lone Dog had her den.

As Kaya came near the den, she called softly, "Here I am, girl, I'm back again." She saw Lone Dog's gold eyes watching her, then the pale tip of her wagging tail. Kaya knelt and parted the grass in front of the nest. The puppies were sleeping in a heap by their mother's side. Lone Dog lifted her head, pricked her ears, and gazed long and hard into Kaya's eyes.

42

"Are you telling me you know I'm sad?" Kaya asked the dog softly. She placed the food into the nest, and Lone Dog ate without getting to her feet, as if she didn't want to disturb her sleeping pups.

After Lone Dog had eaten, Kaya leaned closer and stroked the dog's ears and the soft fur under her jaw. She sank her fingers into the thick coat on her back and scratched. "You always let me touch you now," she said to Lone Dog. "Would you let me touch your puppies? You know I won't hurt them. I'm their friend, too."

Moving slowly, Kaya gently stroked the largest pup's warm head with her fingertip. Would Lone Dog growl her away? Panting lightly, Lone Dog looked on calmly.

Then, as Kaya watched, the pup's eyelids parted for the first time. His milky-blue eyes seemed to be looking right at Kaya, but she knew he was too young to see her yet.

That unseeing gaze reminded Kaya of her blind sister's, and she remembered the lullaby she and Speaking Rain loved so well. "*Ha no nee, ha no nee,*" she sang softly to the puppy. "Here's my precious one, my own, dear little precious one."

As Kaya sang, the other puppies began to stir and whimper, crawling against their mother, wanting more milk. Kaya watched the peaceful scene, the ache in her heart easing. She'd been right to come here.

Crack! A stick broke. Then the long grass bent down and rose again.

Kaya sat up quickly. The twins! She could see the tops of their dark heads in the grass. They were sneaking up the hill, playing hunters with their small bows and arrows.

"Boys!" she hissed. "Stay away! This dog might think you'll hurt her puppies and—"

Wing Feather jumped to his feet. "Puppies!" he cried.

Sparrow sprang upright, too. "Can we see them?" he asked.

Before Kaya could stop them, the boys ran up the slope and fell to their knees beside her. "Keep back!" she said. "Lone Dog doesn't know you!" She held out her arm to keep the boys away from the nest, and they settled down on their heels, gazing wide-eyed at the pups.

"She always protects her puppies," Kaya told

"Ha no nee, ha no nee," Kaya sang softly to the puppy.

the boys. "I'm not sure she'll trust you." If they came too close, would the dog threaten them with a growl, or lunge at them, as she had at Snow Paws?

But Lone Dog didn't seem at all worried by the little boys. Her gaze took them in, then returned to Kaya. Brown Deer had said Lone Dog might have bitten a child or nipped at a baby. *Surely Brown Deer is wrong*, Kaya thought. *Lone Dog knows the twins are no danger to her pups.*

Sparrow was inching closer to the nest. He reached out toward one of the pups, but Kaya caught his hand in hers. "You mustn't touch them," she said firmly.

"Why not?" Wing Feather asked. "Dogs like to be petted."

Kaya thought for a moment. Lone Dog wasn't like the other dogs. Kaya had come to trust Lone Dog, but others thought she might be dangerous, and Kaya couldn't prove that they were wrong. Her grandmother had warned her to be cautious around the dog—and Kaya must take good care of her little brothers, no matter what.

"Listen to me. I want to tell you something," she said to the twins. She hoped her voice sounded like her grandmother's when she commanded attention.

The twins looked up at her right away.

"Lone Dog trusts me," Kaya said. "That's why she lets you two near her puppies. But I'm not sure what she'd do if I weren't with you. To be safe, you mustn't come here by yourselves. Do you hear my warning?" She looked right into their eyes.

After a moment, the little boys nodded.

"Tawts!" she said to them. "Don't forget what I told you. Now come with me. We need to get back to camp."

CHAPTER
FOUR
—

DANGER FOR THE PUPS

Each morning when Kaya awoke, she thought first of Lone Dog. She dressed and left the tepee even before her grandmother began to sing her morning prayers. Kaya loved spending time with the puppies before the work of the day began.

"Tawts-may-we, Lone Dog!" Kaya called softly as she approached the den in the early mist. "It's me again!" Every day a surprise awaited her as the puppies grew and changed.

After the pups had opened their eyes, they learned to use their stubby legs to creep about. Once they could walk around their den, they began sniffing it, too—and sniffing each other. Then their

baby teeth began to show, and chewing on one
another's ears and paws became their pastime. And
soon after they began to chew, their hearing
developed. Now, as Kaya approached them, the
puppies turned toward her voice. The largest pup,
which she called *Tatlo* because he still made
her think of a ground squirrel, peeked
over the side of the nest.

"Are you glad to see me?" Kaya
asked Lone Dog, who lay among her
puppies. Lone Dog's tail wagged as Kaya patted her
and then stroked Tatlo's soft little ears.

As Kaya stroked the three other pups, Lone Dog
jumped out of the nest and took the bone Kaya had
brought her. She carried it off a short way and lay
down to chew on it. She was leaving her puppies
more and more often, though she still stayed nearby
to protect them.

Of course, the puppies didn't like their mother
leaving them, even for a little while. They yipped
and pawed the sides of the nest, trying to call her
back to them. Enjoying her bone, Lone Dog ignored
their whimpers and cries.

"Hush, hush," Kaya crooned to them. "Your

mother needs a rest. She'll come to you soon enough."

With his paws on the edge of the nest, Tatlo watched Lone Dog contentedly munch the bone. The pup impatiently scratched harder and harder, wanting to follow her. Then he got his hind feet going, too, and managed to creep higher. For a moment he teetered on the edge of the nest, then thrust himself over and tumbled out. His high-pitched yelp brought Lone Dog to his side. She licked her startled pup to calm him.

Tatlo's wail excited the other pups to more frantic yipping. Kaya knew that very soon they'd learn how to follow their brother out of the nest. "How will you take care of the pups when they can roam about?" Kaya mused aloud.

Lone Dog's yellow eyes gazed into hers. She seemed to be saying, *I'll teach them to come back to this safe place if there's trouble.*

Kaya scratched Lone Dog behind her ears. "But what if a coyote trails them?" she asked. "What if a bear finds your den?"

Lone Dog nudged Tatlo back into the nest, then jumped in after him. The pups swarmed over their mother as she lay down again to nurse them. She rested on her side, her eyes still on Kaya. She seemed to be saying, *They'll obey me. Wait, you'll see.*

"I'd like to wait," Kaya said. "But I have to join the others now. I'll come back as soon as I can."

Kaya ran all the way to the stream, where the women and girls were splashing in the icy water before taking their morning sweat bath. Beside the sweat lodge, a fire burned on the pile of stones, heating them red-hot. Eetsa was pushing some glowing stones into the lodge to warm it while the others swam. Kaya undressed and joined them.

When everyone had crowded into the dimly lit lodge, Eetsa pulled a deerskin over the doorway. Then she sprinkled cold water onto the heated stones. They sizzled and popped, sending up a cloud of steam. The women and girls joined in a song of thanks and praise to Grandfather Sweat Lodge for helping them and guarding them against illness. Hugging her knees, Kaya sat beside her grandmother.

"I was looking for you, Granddaughter," Kautsa said. "Where were you?" She rubbed her shoulders

51

and arms with the soft tips of the fir branches that covered the floor.

"I went to see the puppies again," Kaya said. Already she felt sweat running off her face and down her back.

"How is the lone dog behaving now?" Kaya's grandmother asked, handing her a handful of the sweet-smelling fir to scrub herself.

"She likes me to visit her," Kaya murmured. Although her grandmother had given her permission to feed Lone Dog, Kaya knew she didn't really trust the dog. "Her pups are getting big and fat."

"Tawts," Kautsa said. "Soon she'll start to wean them. Then they'll join our dog pack—if the lone dog lets them."

Kaya leaned closer to her grandmother. "Sometimes Lone Dog seems to be talking to me with her eyes," she whispered. "Do you believe me?"

"Aa-heh!" Kautsa said right away. "I believe you. Animals talk to us in many, many ways."

"But I mean she really *speaks* to me, too," Kaya whispered even more softly.

Kautsa sat with her head bent, silently breathing in the cleansing steam. After a time, she said, "I'm thinking about my mother. When she was a girl, she received a wolf spirit, and after that she could talk with wolves. One day, when she was very old, a wolf trotted along the trail where she was picking berries. The wolf was sad because her puppies had died. My mother was very sorry for the wolf. She asked the wolf if she could help her. The wolf told her that she was leaving the mountains, and refused help. But then she gave my mother the gift of her wolf power. That power made my mother even stronger."

"The wolf spoke to her?" Kaya asked. "Like Lone Dog speaks to me?"

"All creatures have wisdom to share with us," Kautsa said. "Soon you'll prepare for your vision quest, and I hope you'll receive a *wyakin* of your own. If you do, you must always listen closely to what it tells you."

"Aa-heh!" Kaya said. With all her heart, she hoped to be ready for her vision quest. Would she receive wolf power, as her great-grandmother had? As Kaya tried to imagine that, Eetsa pulled aside the deerskin covering the door and signaled everyone to leave the steamy lodge and plunge into the stream again.

⟁

"You're too old to quarrel like this!" Kaya said to the twins. "Listen to me and do as I say!" She held Wing Feather by one hand and Sparrow by the other. The little boys had been wrestling playfully on the hillside when their game suddenly became too rough.

Sparrow tried to pull his hand from her grasp.

Wing Feather scowled. "We lost most of our arrows," he said. "If you make us some more, I promise we won't fight over them."

"Aa-heh," Kaya said. "If you sit there quietly, I'll make more arrows for you." She sighed as she cut some straight twigs from an elderberry bush. Her little brothers were full of energy and full of tricks. Eetsa told Kaya to take care of them even more often now that she couldn't dig roots with the other girls and women.

But the twins didn't pay enough attention to Kaya's warnings. Kaya wished she could teach the boys to obey her as easily as Lone Dog had taught her pups. Usually it took the dog no more than a soft growl or a shake to bring her troublesome pups in line again.

Like the twins, the pups romped and wrestled and tugged and chased one another all day. But sometimes Lone Dog gave a special growl that meant, *Take cover!* Then they tumbled back into the den, where they were safe from bobcats, or an eagle hovering overhead. *She's taught her pups well*, Kaya thought as she finished cutting notches in the arrows.

"Here, boys," Kaya said. "I've made two arrows for each of you. You can go hunting again."

Wing Feather had fallen asleep on the soft grass, his hand tucked into his baby moccasin, which he always kept with him. He rolled onto his back and rubbed his eyes with it. "Katsee-yow-yow!" he said, reaching for the little arrows.

Kaya looked around for Sparrow. He'd been lying on his stomach by his brother, but now he was nowhere to be seen.

"Is that bothersome boy hiding from me again?" Kaya asked Wing Feather. "I have to find him. Do you know which way he might have gone?"

Wing Feather's lower lip stuck out. "He should have waited for me. I told him we couldn't visit the puppies without you, but he—"

Puppies! Kaya's pulse sped. She imagined Sparrow sneaking up on Lone Dog's den, determined to touch the pups. She didn't believe that Lone Dog would hurt the boy, but she couldn't be certain. She knew only that she had to get to her brother as fast as she could. "Come on!" she said. She grabbed Wing Feather's hand and started running.

Kaya and her little brother rushed down the path alongside the stream. Then they turned and ran up the long, steep hillside. Lone Dog's den was on the far side of the hill, hidden from view by underbrush.

Kaya paused on the crest of the hill to look for

Sparrow. In a moment, she saw him coming around the base of the hill below her. He was running as silently as a shadow, as he'd been taught. He was going to get to the den before she could. Would Lone Dog chase him away with a nip?

Kaya could barely make out the entrance of the den. Something dark moved there, but it didn't look like a dog. Then Kaya realized that a bear was digging at the opening of the den, trying to get at the hidden puppies! And, running uphill, Sparrow wouldn't be able to see the bear until he'd reached the clearing!

"Stay here!" Kaya commanded Wing Feather, and she took off racing for the den as fast as she could. But it was like running in a bad dream—her feet felt as if they were weighted with stones. She didn't shout for Sparrow to stay back because she didn't want to startle the bear—if it turned on her little brother, it could kill him with a single swipe of its sharp claws!

Then the bear heard Sparrow coming. It swung around and lumbered away from the den, its huge head swaying, its jaws wide. Just at that moment,

Sparrow burst into the clearing. He saw the bear and skidded to a halt. Then he scrambled toward the den as if he wanted to crawl into it with the puppies. But there was no way for him to hide from the bear, which was heading right for him!

A SAD PARTING

A pale streak flew by Kaya and plunged down the hill toward the den—it was Lone Dog! She was barking ferociously with alarm, her teeth bared and her hackles raised. With a long leap, she hurled herself down at the bear. She snapped viciously at its heels and lunged at its flanks. The bear rose onto its hind legs, swatting at Lone Dog, trying to grab her with its claws. There was blood on Lone Dog's back and shoulders, but she kept up her fierce attack. She was determined to protect her pups—and Sparrow—even if it meant her life.

Kaya ran into the clearing. She yelled as loudly as she could, waving her arms over her head.

The bear looked her way. It went down on all fours again and backed off a little, confused by the noise. Then it chose not to fight. As it turned away, Lone Dog continued to bite at its heels, moving it along until it had disappeared into the thick underbrush and was gone. Still barking, Lone Dog dashed back to the den and her puppies.

Kaya ran to Sparrow. Hugging himself, he crouched against the hillside. He was crying. Kaya threw her arms around her little brother and held him close.

Wing Feather came leaping down the slope. "I saw it all!" he called out as he came. "Lone Dog fought just like a wolf! She saved her puppies, and she saved Sparrow, too!"

"Aa-heh, you're safe now!" Kaya tipped up Sparrow's chin so she could look him in the eye. "But if it hadn't been for Lone Dog, you wouldn't have had a chance against that bear. You owe your life to a very brave dog."

⟁

A few days later, Kaya piled some deerskins onto a travois and hitched it to the gray horse.

"You owe your life to a very brave dog," Kaya told Sparrow.

The gentle gray's hoof was healed, and she accepted the travois as if she'd always pulled one—Kaya's training had been good. As Kaya rode out to the dog den on the hillside, she considered her plan. Lone Dog had weaned her pups, and Kaya knew they were at an age when they should get accustomed to other dogs and to people, too. She thought that if she took the pups to the village with her, maybe she could lure Lone Dog to follow. She hoped Lone Dog would live by their tepee and be her special dog now.

The pups were prancing about in front of the den. Tatlo had a small bone in his mouth, and the other three pups were chasing after him, trying to get it. When his little sister managed to pry it away, Tatlo rolled her onto her back and buried his face in her neck, growling. She pawed at Tatlo's face. They seemed to be fighting, but their tails were wagging.

Lone Dog lay on the hillside above the den, her head resting on her paws. With the help of a poultice of *wapalwaapal* that Kaya had made, her wounds were healing well. When Kaya slid off the horse, Lone Dog got to her feet and stretched. Then she came to lean affectionately against Kaya's legs. Kaya scratched her back just above her tail. "Your pups are growing fast, aren't they?" Kaya said to her friend. "Now they can become part of our dog pack."

Lone Dog looked toward her pups wrestling for the bone, then back at Kaya. Would this solitary dog allow her pups to live among people?

"And I hope you'll come to live with me, too," Kaya said softly.

Lone Dog looked away. After a moment, she went back to the hillside and lay down again. She seemed to be thinking over what Kaya had said.

Kaya rounded up the puppies and put them into the makeshift nest on the travois. They curled up together, as if pleased to be going on a ride. Kaya mounted the horse and called, "Come, Lone Dog! Come!" Hoping that Lone Dog would follow, she began to ride slowly toward the path that led to the village. When she glanced over her shoulder, Lone Dog was trotting down the hillside to follow them.

But Kaya's worries were far from over. Everyone trusted Lone Dog since she'd saved Sparrow, but Kaya wasn't sure what Snow Paws would do when he saw Lone Dog approach the village. Would he still think she was a danger? In an all-out fight, he could injure or kill her. As Kaya rode toward the tepees, she watched warily for the big black dog.

Soon Snow Paws came barking loudly to confront Lone Dog. He took a stand near the tepees and set himself to defend the village.

Kautsa was making finger cakes with some other women. "Snow Paws, go!" she commanded the dog. "Go!" she repeated even more loudly. "Lone Dog belongs here now!"

Snow Paws stopped barking, but he approached Lone Dog slowly on stiff legs. Lone Dog stood perfectly still, her ears slightly back—she was in his territory now. He sniffed her, then allowed her to sniff him in return. When he walked back to the other dogs, Kaya knew he had accepted Lone Dog as one of the pack. Oh, she hoped Lone Dog would stay with her here in the village!

⚜

Kautsa was stringing dried roots and dried kouse cakes on hemp cord so they could be carried easily when it was time to travel again. Kaya worked at her grandmother's side, cutting the cord into even lengths and handing the pieces to her as she needed them.

The season for digging roots here was coming to an end. Soon everyone would leave the Palouse Prairie and journey to the meadows to dig camas there. Kaya knew the camas plants were already in bloom, their deep blue flowers making the meadows look like vast, shimmering lakes. And soon it would be time for the spring salmon runs, too. Kaya loved to travel, but now she worried that Lone Dog might not follow her when they broke camp, although her pups had joined the dog pack.

camas plant

Lone Dog didn't seem to be at ease around people or the other dogs. When Kaya was in the camp, Lone Dog stayed near her side. But when Kaya left the camp for wood or water, Lone Dog ran off by herself into the hills, sometimes staying away all night.

"Is something troubling you, Granddaughter?" Kautsa asked. She held out her hand for another piece of cord.

"Aa-heh," Kaya admitted. "Do you remember I told you that Lone Dog sometimes speaks to me?"

"What does Lone Dog tell you these days?" Kautsa asked.

"I think she's saying that she's going to leave us," Kaya said. "She's not meant to be a village dog."

Kautsa nodded. "It's true that she's different from our other dogs. Perhaps it's her nature to live alone."

"But I don't want her to leave me!" Kaya burst out. "I want her to be my dog always!"

Kautsa thought for a while. Then she picked up the ball of hemp cord and held it out to Kaya. "You could tie this rope around her neck so she couldn't run off. Have you thought of doing that?"

Kaya frowned in concentration. She tried to think what Swan Circling would do. "If I tied up Lone Dog, she'd be the same as a captive, wouldn't she?" she asked miserably. "The enemies from Buffalo Country tied me up every night. The rope kept me from running away, but I was desperate to escape. Lone Dog would feel the same way. I couldn't do that to her. I couldn't!"

Her grandmother put her warm hand on Kaya's shoulder. "Listen to me. I have something to tell you."

Kaya looked up at her grandmother, who was gazing at her with love and concern. "I know it will be hard for you to let Lone Dog go her own way," Kautsa said thoughtfully. "But, as you said yourself, someone who has been a captive understands the powerful need to be free. Can you respect what's best for her?"

Kaya bit her lip. She didn't want to imagine her life without Lone Dog in it.

On the morning the women began to pack up all their belongings for the journey to the camas meadows, Kaya went looking for Lone Dog. She hadn't seen the dog since the men had rounded up the horses the day before and brought them to camp to be loaded for the trip. Kaya looked all around the camp, calling her name. Where was she? Was she up there on the ridge? Kaya ran up to the top, then over the hill to the abandoned den on the far side. She saw the striped face of a badger that had taken over the empty den. But Lone Dog was nowhere to be seen.

Kaya remembered that sometimes

Lone Dog had been gone for longer than this. But by the time the women had rolled up all the tule mats and stashed the tepee poles to be used the next year, Lone Dog was still missing.

Raven came by, leading some pack horses. "I hear your dog's run off," he said, but he didn't sound pleased about it.

"She isn't *my* dog," Kaya said, as firmly as she could. "She belongs to herself. Anyway, she might follow us later." But in her heart, Kaya knew that Lone Dog had gone on her way—alone—as she needed to be.

Don't cry! Kaya told herself. *Keep good thoughts!* But her throat was tight with tears.

As Kaya was helping the twins climb onto a travois, she felt a tug at the hem of her dress. It was Tatlo, pulling at her skirt and begging to play.

When Kaya ignored him, he began to sniff the bundles piled up near the horses. She heard him give his puppy growl, then saw him drag something from one of the bundles. With another growl, he started shaking what he'd found—it was Speaking Rain's doll!

"Tatlo, that's not a toy for you!" Kaya cried.

"Bring that to me!" She knew if she chased him, he'd run away from her with the precious doll. So she sat on the ground to encourage him to come closer. He paused, his head cocked. Then he trotted to her and dropped the doll into her lap, his whole body wiggling as if he knew he'd done something good.

"Tawts, Tatlo!" Kaya said. She pushed the doll behind her and lifted the pup onto her lap. "Are you telling me you're going to help me find my sister someday?" she asked him.

Tatlo put his paws on her shoulders and looked at her with his amber eyes. Then he nipped at her braids and licked her cheek and her chin. Kaya couldn't help but laugh as the rough little tongue tickled her face.

"Jump down, now," Kaya told him. But instead of jumping down, Tatlo turned around and around until he'd curled up in her lap. As soon as he laid his head on Kaya's legs, he was asleep.

Kaya gently stroked the sleeping puppy. His muzzle was pale, like Lone Dog's, and his big paws meant he'd grow to be large, like her. "I think your mother sent you to be my dog now," Kaya whispered to him. "We have a long, long way to travel, and I'll be very glad to have you with me."

A PEEK INTO
THE PAST

When a baby was born in Kaya's time, the whole village rejoiced in the new life beginning. The elder who was in charge of remembering all births, deaths, marriages, and other kinships for the village proudly announced the new baby's place among the extended family.

The name a Nez Perce mother gave her baby at birth often reflected her hopes and dreams for the baby. Kaya's mother named her Kaya'aton'my' for the first thing she saw after giving birth—a woman arranging rocks to heat a sweat lodge. Women with healing powers often performed this task, and Eetsa wanted Kaya to be like them. A child received new names throughout life, sometimes to mark an especially brave deed or life-shaping event, or sometimes because an older relative wanted a child to have her name, just as Swan Circling gave her name to Kaya.

A baby laced into a cradleboard

Babies were never far from their mothers and other female relatives. They spent much of their first year laced snugly into cradleboards. The bottom of the cradleboard was lined with soft, absorbent moss or cattail fluff—a

The gentle sway of a horse's walk usually rocked a baby right to sleep.

natural diaper for the baby. Since Nez Perces were so often on the move, cradleboards made it easy for mothers and other relatives to carry babies with them—even when they rode on horseback. Cradleboards had loops that easily slipped over the pommel, or high handle, of a saddle.

As soon as babies could toddle, elders began encouraging the gifts they saw in each child—athletics, leadership, healing, hunting, music, horsemanship, and many other talents. Each of these gifts was valued by the community and essential for its survival.

When a child was about five years old, her official training began. She was awakened every morning at dawn by her female elders and taken to the river for a cold bath and swim with all the other girls in the village. Then they ran long distances to build strength and endurance. Each day, all the girls filed into the sweat lodge to cleanse the impurities from their bodies and their spirits.

Elders prepared children to be strong and resourceful.

Elders watched the children closely for signs of readiness for certain ceremonies, or rites of passage. An important ceremony for Nez Perce girls happened early each summer, when camas bulbs were ready to be harvested. The first time a girl dug bulbs as a working member of the group, she had the honor of serving them to the eldest women of the village. The girl did not eat during this ceremony, to show that she was now a provider. After the feast, elders often gave speeches to encourage and praise the girl, and blessed her work. She might also receive a new name at this ceremony.

As children grew older, elders prepared them for the most important event in their lives—their vision quest. When children reached the age of 12 or 13, they were sent alone into the mountains or another isolated spot for several days to seek a spirit helper, or wyakin.

Today, woven hats are worn by women only for special occasions and ceremonies. In Kaya's time, women wore them as everyday hats.

During their vigil they ate no food and drank little water. If they had prepared themselves well, a wyakin would come to them first as a human being and present a certain power, such as the skill to find roots easily or the ability to hunt with great accuracy. Then the wyakin would take the form of something in nature—an animal, a plant, or even a sunset or the wind—revealing its true character. People might collect several wyakins throughout their lives. Young people who had already collected several wyakins often became *shamans*, or powerful healers.

After a child received a wyakin, that wyakin was always available to him or her. A person with buffalo power might be called on when a buffalo hunt wasn't going well. She would call to her spirit and try to persuade the buffalo to come back to her people.

Nez Perce children were taught to honor and respect all creatures. Whenever deer were killed or fish were caught, the whole village thanked the animals for giving themselves to their people for food.

Delia Lowry was a powerful shaman.

Nez Perce Indians believe that long ago, animals talked just as humans do. The only reason animals no longer talk is that humans stopped listening to them.

Nez Perces always had animals near them. They began bonding with horses from the moment their cradleboards first swung from a saddle. Young girls helped make decorated horse trappings for special occasions and ceremonies. Flowing saddlebag fringes hung nearly to the ground and swayed gracefully as the horse walked. Dangling shells on horse collars jingled in time with the horse's trot. Small feathers or beads embellished bridles. Each horse was dressed as uniquely as the girl who rode it.

Village dogs were loyal and trusted protectors, workers, and companions. When women rode out to collect roots or berries or even daily firewood, their faithful dogs always came with them. The dogs' keen sense of smell gave them the power to warn the women of predators before

Girls Kaya's age and younger were already expert riders. They often owned their own horses that they trained themselves.

Nez Perces' love and respect for animals lasts a lifetime.

they could be seen. In days before the Nez Perces had horses, children who were old enough to walk traveled with pack dogs in front of and behind them, to protect them.

Today, one of the ways the Nez Perce people continue to honor their bond with animals is through their Wolf Reintroduction Program. Wolves are now an endangered species, and the Nez Perce Tribe cares for several packs, hoping to ensure their survival. The Wolf Education Center also operates on Nez Perce land. Visitors can take guided hikes to see the 20-acre enclosure of wolves, if the wolves choose to be seen. The wolves are especially playful and tender when children visit them. Wolves adore children, and puppies. When wolf pups are born, the adults chase and frolic and howl, rejoicing in new life and announcing it to the pack, in much the same way Nez Perce elders proudly announced new births to their villages long ago.

Today, wolves sometimes make school visits!

GLOSSARY OF NEZ PERCE WORDS

In the story, Nez Perce words are spelled so that English readers can pronounce them. Here, you can also see how the words are actually spelled and said by the Nez Perce people.

Phonetic/Nez Perce	Pronunciation	Meaning
aa-heh/'éehe	*AA-heh*	yes, that's right
Eetsa/Iice	*EET-sah*	Mother
Hun-ya-wat/ Hanyaw'áat	*hun-yah-WAHT*	the Creator
katsee-yow-yow/ qe'ci'yew'yew'	*KAHT-see-yow-yow*	thank you
Kautsa/Qáaca'c	*KOUT-sah*	grandmother from mother's side
Kaya'aton'my'	*ky-YAAH-ton-my*	she who arranges rocks
Nimíipuu	*Nee-MEE-poo*	The People; known today as the Nez Perce Indians
Pi-lah-ka/Piláqá	*pee-LAH-kah*	grandfather from mother's side
Salish/Sélix	*SAY-leesh*	friends of the Nez Perce who live near them
Tatlo	*TAHT-lo*	ground squirrel
tawts/ta'c	*TAWTS*	good
tawts may-we/ ta'c méeywi	*TAWTS MAY-wee*	good morning
Toe-ta/Toot'a	*TOH-tah*	Father

Wallowa/ **Wal'áwa**	*wah-LAU-wa*	Wallowa Valley in present-day Oregon
wapalwaapal	*WAH-pul-WAAH-pul*	western yarrow, a plant that helps stop bleeding
wyakin/ **wéeyekin**	*WHY-ah-kin*	guardian spirit

THE BOOKS ABOUT KAYA

MEET KAYA • An American Girl
Kaya's boasting gets her into big trouble
and earns her a terrible nickname.

KAYA'S ESCAPE! • A Survival Story
Kaya and her sister, Speaking Rain, are captured in
an enemy raid. Can they find a way to escape?

KAYA'S HERO • A Story of Giving
Kaya becomes close friends with a warrior
woman named Swan Circling, who inspires
Kaya and gives her an amazing gift.

KAYA AND LONE DOG • A Friendship Story
Kaya befriends a lone dog, who teaches her
about love and letting go.

KAYA SHOWS THE WAY • A Sister Story
Kaya is reunited with Speaking Rain, who has
a surprising decision to share.

CHANGES FOR KAYA • A Story of Courage
Kaya and her horse, Steps High, are caught
in a flash fire. Can they outrun it?

Coming in Spring 2003
WELCOME TO KAYA'S WORLD • 1764
History is lavishly illustrated with
photographs, illustrations, and artifacts
of the Nez Perce people.

MORE TO DISCOVER!

While books are the heart of The American Girls Collection,® they are only the beginning. The stories in the Collection come to life when you act them out with the beautiful American Girls dolls and their exquisite clothes and accessories. To request a free catalogue full of things girls love, send in this postcard, call **1-800-845-0005,** or visit our Web site at **americangirl.com**.

Please send me an American Girl®catalogue.

My name is ⎯⎯⎯⎯⎯⎯⎯⎯⎯⎯⎯⎯⎯⎯⎯⎯⎯⎯⎯⎯⎯⎯⎯⎯

My address is ⎯⎯⎯⎯⎯⎯⎯⎯⎯⎯⎯⎯⎯⎯⎯⎯⎯⎯⎯⎯⎯⎯

City ⎯⎯⎯⎯⎯⎯⎯⎯⎯⎯⎯⎯⎯ State ⎯⎯⎯⎯⎯ Zip ⎯⎯⎯⎯⎯

My birth date is ⎯⎯⎯/⎯⎯⎯/⎯⎯⎯ E-mail address ⎯⎯⎯⎯⎯⎯⎯⎯
             month   day   year   *Fill in to receive updates and web-exclusive offers.*

Parent's signature ⎯⎯⎯⎯⎯⎯⎯⎯⎯⎯⎯⎯⎯⎯⎯⎯⎯⎯⎯⎯

And send a catalogue to my friend.

My friend's name is ⎯⎯⎯⎯⎯⎯⎯⎯⎯⎯⎯⎯⎯⎯⎯⎯⎯⎯

Address ⎯⎯⎯⎯⎯⎯⎯⎯⎯⎯⎯⎯⎯⎯⎯⎯⎯⎯⎯⎯⎯⎯⎯⎯⎯

City ⎯⎯⎯⎯⎯⎯⎯⎯⎯⎯⎯⎯⎯ State ⎯⎯⎯⎯⎯ Zip ⎯⎯⎯⎯⎯

If the postcard has already been removed from this book and you would like to receive an American Girl® catalogue, please send your name and address to:

American Girl
P.O. Box 620497
Middleton, WI 53562-0497

You may also call our toll-free number, **1-800-845-0005,** or visit our Web site at **americangirl.com**.

Place
Stamp
Here

PO BOX 620497
MIDDLETON WI 53562-0497